Rosella of The Darkness World and her Live-forever Potion

Elena Sommers

Rosella of The Darkness World
and her Live-forever Potion

Elena Sommers

Illustration Raphilena Bonito
Design ©Tricorn Books
www.tricornbooks.co.uk

ISBN 9781909660960

Published 2018 by Tricorn Books
28 Landport Terrace, Portsmouth PO1 2RG

Rosella of The Darkness World
and her
Live-forever Potion

Chapter 1

Darkness World

Once upon a time there was a gloomy, creepy, cold, enchanted black stone castle surrounded by the impenetrable dark woods.

The crooked bare branches twisted and turned in all directions creating a strange pattern. The black water of the lake, full of frogs and lizards, reflected in the moonlight behind the castle. The captivating, magical moving lights surrounded that castle – like stars in the sky distracting all strangers. The black flying horses grazed nearby impatiently waiting for their owners.

The young, powerful Queen of The Darkness World, Rosella, lived there. Her unusual friends, Fire, Water and Gravity, visited her occasionally to make mysterious magic.

The witches and wizards lived in these woods in the driving and talking wooden huts, which crept and squeaked all the time. A large, rectangular boarding school, made of brown bricks stood nearby. It was full of children who studied science and magic.

The talking black cats jumped up and down the trees to show each other their magic. The wild, black talking crows circled round the woods creating a creepy chaos.

All strangers were forbidden to come in or out, the country was under a dark magic spell.

Everything about this country was dark and mysterious.

Chapter 2

Rosella

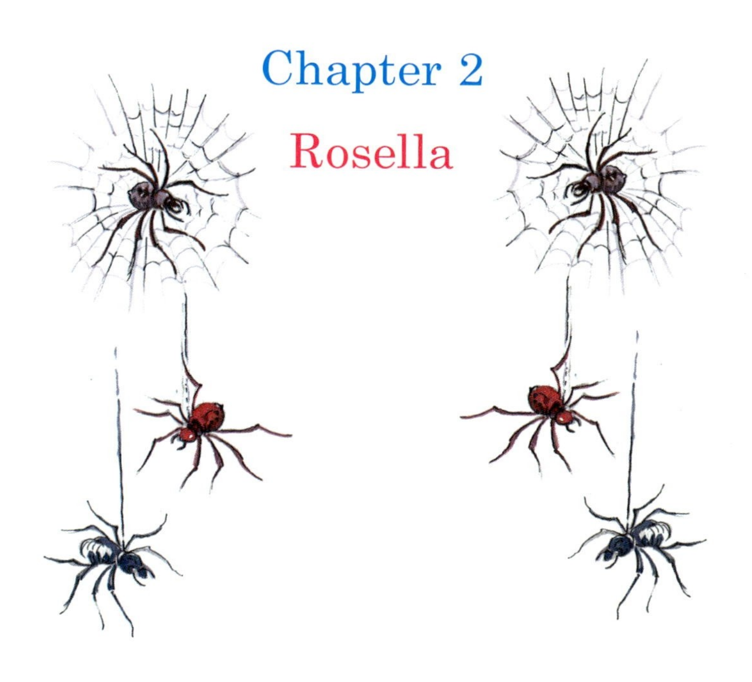

Inside the castle looked even spookier. An enormous hot blazing fire crackled fiercely in a huge fireplace in a tall, round, echoing hall. The creepy old spiders hung around the castle in enchanted patterns. These talking spiders whispered to each other, sharing their magical secrets.

The black talking crows
circled around the ceiling,
screeching loudly in the hall.
A chunky cauldron bubbled
fiercely in the middle. It was full of
gluey black liquid. A pile of bottles,
flasks and jars with weird writing
stood untidily on a table.

They were full of
different coloured liquid.
A few scruffy old magic
books were scattered
around the floor. A pile
of red poisoned apples,
pumpkins and herbs were
in the corner.

A fat talking black cat
named Night mixed a few
herbs near the fire creating
a cloud of dust.

Rosella stood near the
cauldron reading a floating-
in-the-air magical book and
held her diamond mobile
mirror.

She was a powerful Queen of her country; everyone had to obey her orders. Her silky black long dress and black cloak swept the floor when she walked. Her diamond crown with rubies sparkled magically all the time in contrast with her pretty, silky black hair. Rosella was quite a strong enchantress. She knew many powerful spells and even forbidden magic. The thing that she wanted most of all was to be young and be alive forever. She wished to find a formula for a live-forever potion. So far, she was not in luck. Her old friends Water, Fire and Gravity helped her with her search.

Chapter 3

Mobile mirror

Next morning Rosella stood near the cauldron holding her diamond mobile mirror, Lexa. It could ask and answer questions, tell stories, show pictures, play music and even more. It looked a bit like a normal mobile phone with a handle. The Queen was always with it.

‘Good morning, Rosella.

What would you like to discover today?’ asked the mirror loudly.

‘Tell me, Lexa, what ingredients do you need to make a live-forever potion?’ she answered.

‘My knowledge is incomplete. You need five ingredients: two poisoned apples, one pumpkin, a pot of the hottest lava, a ring of life and something else I don’t know.’

‘Excellent, Lexa. We’re nearly there. I have two ingredients already – pumpkins and poisoned apples. I know the fifth ingredient too.’

'What is the fifth ingredient, your Majesty?' the cat asked blowing triangle bubbles.

'Be quiet, Night!' she ordered. 'The fifth ingredient is a tiny bit of happiness taken from 1,000 children.'

'Where are you going to find 1,000 children, Rosella?' Lexa asked in reply.

'Silence!' she squeaked. 'I'll think about it. Where is the ring of life?'

'It's at the bottom of the lake near the castle in the country called Philiphia.'

'Philiphia is the country where I was born,' she said into her mobile mirror. 'Ask Water to visit me. I have a request for her.'

Chapter 4
Water

A few seconds later Water appeared in front of them shimmering like a diamond. She was wearing a long, outfit of all shades of blue. She looked like a walking and talking waterfall. Her own golden wishing fish was floating around in circles on top of her head in a large, floating water bubble. Water was immortal. Also, she was an amphibian. She could be underwater or on land as long as she wished. She also could control the water flow and start and stop thunderstorms.

‘Did you call me, Rosella?’ she smiled. ‘I haven’t seen you for a long time.’

‘Yes. Water, I have a tiny request for you. Go to the country called Philiphia and bring me a ring of life. It’s at the bottom of the round lake. The mermaids protect it. The lake is right in front of the royal castle. I will pay well,’ she asked impatiently.

‘I wonder why, Rosella, do you need it?’ she asked in reply, and her golden wishing fish twisted and turned in its bubble.

‘For live-forever potion. Why is it your concern? I will pay well. What would you like in return?’ Rosella looked firm.

‘A red ruby from Mars with triple power magic,’ Water answered in turn.

‘No! It’s the most powerful item that I own!’ Rosella looked slightly concerned.

‘Rosella, you will be immortal like one of us, a goddess or a force of nature,’ Water replied in a dramatic turn.

'Fine, Water! I will give it to you when you return with the ring of life,' she announced. 'Now leave me alone.' Water waved and vanished in a puff of blue misty smoke.

'Don't drown, Water,' Night mumbled with an enormous smile, when she left and a red firework burst on top of his head.

'Shut up, Night!' Rosella laughed and the blackbird landed on her shoulder.

Chapter 5

Fire

Suddenly, Fire appeared in front of them. He looked exactly like walking and talking lava and a fire monarch. He had a dark red and orange jacket with glowing stones and long glittery boots. He knew the power of fire.

He could go in and out of fire and it didn't harm him. Many things in his castles were made of fire. Two wonderful firebirds sat on his shoulders. The birds had green, yellow, red and blue fire flames in their feathers.

'Hello, your Majesty Rosella the Queen of The Darkness World,' he announced loudly and gave her one of the birds.

‘Thank you, Fire the Greatest, The King of Lavenia. It looks awesome.’ She smiled.

‘The bird’s name is Flame. It brings luck to its owner, it is immortal and it has a beautiful singing voice,’ he explained.

‘I wish I was immortal, like you,’ Rosella answered quietly. ‘I am in the process of making a live-forever potion. Would you like to help?’ she asked with a tremble in her voice.

‘Of course, your Majesty, anything for your smile.’

‘I need a pot of the hottest lava on earth, your Majesty,’ she answered with a grin.

‘Rosella, you are the one for me. I love you. Would you like to be my girlfriend?’ He looked a bit shy.

‘I have to be immortal to accept. Fire, ask me again in the future.’

‘I will go and bring a pot of lava for you, Rosella, as soon as I can.’

They waved goodbye and he vanished in a ball of fire.

Only Flame the bird remained in her hands. She stood there and looked at it for a while, thinking. The bird sung beautifully something nice. Then, her cat Night performed a magical dance with ten flying brooms.

‘Bravo, Night! You are on fire!’ She said goodnight and vanished in a puff of purple smoke.

Chapter 6

Gravity

Next morning Rosella invited Gravity to share her breakfast with him. Gravity looked like an old man.

He had an enormous power to attract things towards him.

Any objects, light or heavy, could fly in his direction, at his command. He was all in grey. Gravity was wearing a grey colour suit, grey cap and a grey shiny pair of shoes.

A rolled-up newspaper was always with him and no one knew the reason. He was immortal and his talking pet wolf named Press never left his beloved master.

Gravity had a deep croaky voice when he spoke. Usually, ordinary people were tired and sleepy in his company. However, over the years Rosella learned how to be friends with him. She simply treated him like he was her grandad.

'It was kind of you to invite me for breakfast, your Majesty,' he started slowly. 'What is on your mind?'

'Nothing special. It's just that I would like to be immortal like you. So, I am in the process of making a live-forever potion. I need a bit of happiness from 1,000 children. Can you use your gravitational force?' She sat there waiting for an answer.

'Awesome flying pumpkin cakes,' he

said. 'I can help you Rosella, for a little reward.'

His wolf stretched and yawned showing his white teeth. One cake flew right into his mouth and he started to catch them non-stop, making everyone laugh.

'I would like a grey triple-power moonstone as my reward,' he said finally.

'Awesome! Deal!' Rosella squeaked in reply.

'How many children do you have in your boarding school, your Majesty?' he asked in his deep voice, catching another cake.

‘725, with new ones.’

‘I can take tiny bits of their happiness, with a pink memory stick, without them even noticing. The tiny spiderwebs of information will be collected from their heads into that stick using my gravitational force.’

‘Awesome what about the other 275 children?’ she asked impatiently.

‘We will think about it later. Thank you for breakfast, it was fabulous. Press especially loves the cakes.’ They laughed, waved then he vanished in a puff of silver smoke.

Chapter 7

Water's adventure

Meanwhile, Water arrived in Philiphia under an invisibility charm. Nobody was able to see her, even mermaids. She decided to explore the round lake first. There was a cute little mermaid city named Rocky, and Poseidon was in charge there. The city looked really pretty.

It had a small shell-shaped white castle in the middle and a few small shell-shaped pink and yellow little houses around it. The mermaids and mermen, in colourful costumes, floated around it, minding their business.

Shiny, golden and silver fish swam backwards and forwards beautifully, in a shoal.

The seaweed decorated the city throughout, creating an enchanted appearance. Water decided to search the town in order to find a ring of life, but no matter how hard she tried, she failed. The mermaids hid it so well, that even being invisible Water wasn't able to find it. She had to change the plan, and fast.

She didn't want to use the last, seventh wish of her wishing fish to find that ring. It had got dark and because she was there for so long killer whales sensed her being there. All of them attacked her at once.

She had no choice except to climb out. She scrambled on to the beach and sat there thinking for a few moments. The moon was bright like a pancake.

'I am not going back there ever again,' she said to herself firmly. 'I have to use my last wish after all'.

'Can you hear me, wishing fish?' she whispered.

'Yes, master,' the fish whispered back.

'Deliver a ring of life to my friend Rosella the Queen,' she whispered.

'All done, master. The ring is delivered to Rosella the Queen. It's time for me to have a new master. Who is my new master from now on?' the fish whispered in one go.

'Rosella is your new master, when she is immortal. You have to wait for a bit.' Water stood up and disappeared in a blue misty smoke.

Next morning, Rosella woke up and found a silver luminously bright little box with a ring of life on her pillow.

A huge smile appeared on her face. She tried to open the box with her trembling hands and the simple charm, but nothing happened.

Then she took her purple wand and directed a light of energy into the box. Finally, the box opened and she saw a little golden ring with a large ruby.

A force of enormous power illuminated dazzlingly from the ring.

'I wonder what is its secret?' she mumbled. Then Rosella put a few different protective charms on it and went down for breakfast.

'Water is my true friend,' she thought to herself. 'She definitely deserved her reward.'

Rosella ordered her cat, Night, to wrap and deliver a red ruby from Mars with triple magic directly to Water.

Chapter 8

Fire's adventure

Fire arrived back to his country, Lavinia, constantly thinking about Rosella. His heart was thumping fast and he imagined her in his mind again and again. Lavinia looked rather picturesque and amazingly pretty. A red, tall, pyramid-shaped castle stood proudly in the middle, it was made from a volcanic crater.

Smaller-sized, black, brown, orange, yellow, pyramid-shaped, made-of-volcanic-craters houses stood proudly around the castle.

Four beautiful lava lakes were placed around the castle. The first lake was bright pink, the second lake was ruby red, the third lake was blindingly turquoise and the fourth lake was deep purple.

The surface of the country had orange sand, like in the desert. Hot geysers of chocolate were scattered around the town, inviting everyone to try some.

Flying fire horses grazed looking for scrumptious cacti. Firebirds were sitting on top of the pyramids, singing or flying around, playing chase.

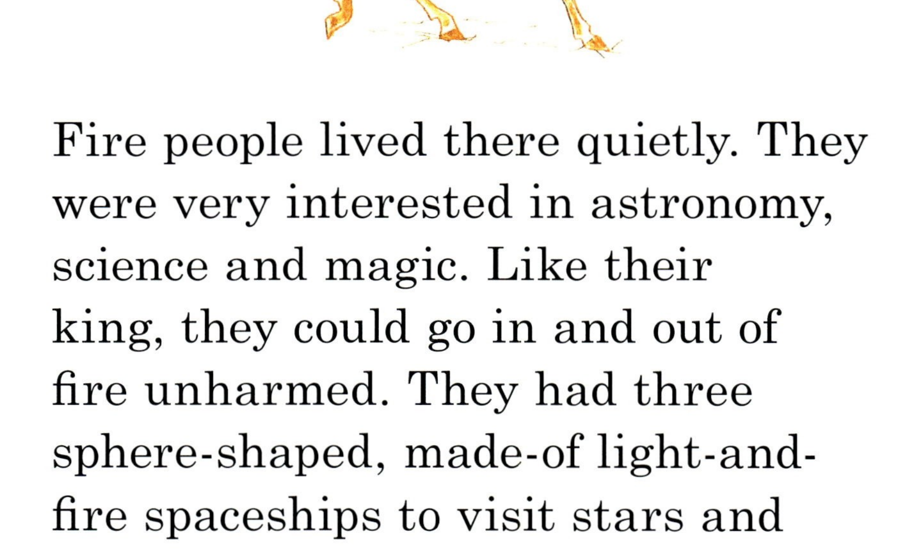

Fire people lived there quietly. They were very interested in astronomy, science and magic. Like their king, they could go in and out of fire unharmed. They had three sphere-shaped, made-of light-and-fire spaceships to visit stars and planets, whenever they wished.

Fire had something else on his mind. He took a fireproof pot and had a fast ride on his favourite flying horse towards a red lava lake. Then he decided to walk round looking for the hottest lava on earth. The lava bubbled and scattered flames. He walked right into the middle of the lake, using special magic not to be sucked in.

Then he placed the pot, using its handle, into bubbling lava and collected some. Then he closed the pot tight and decided to deliver it straight to Rosella. He climbed out of the lake, and took a long ride on his flying horse. He couldn't stop thinking about her. Rosella was always on his mind.

When he arrived in her castle, she was in her large orangery or herbology room made of glass. It was full of exotic and ordinary plants. The room was very light and hot. The magical colourful birds of paradise were flying round and round. Rosella was wearing a long, silky green dress. She didn't expect to see Fire.

'Hello Rosella the Queen of The Darkness World, I brought you a pot of lava,' he announced loudly.

'Thank you, Fire. It's so fantastic. Not long until I will be immortal.' She smiled. They looked directly into each other's eyes for quite a while, holding hands.

'I love you Rosella,' he whispered.

'I love you too, Fire.' Then they had their first kiss. 'Flame the bird brings me luck.' They stood there talking for a few minutes and colourful birds of paradise flew above their heads.

Chapter 9

Gravity and his job

First, Gravity went into Rosella's boarding school. It was made of brown bricks. The classrooms were spacious, full of light and a lot of magical books and fascinating study material.

The children studied the beginning of magic, science, chemistry, biology and astronomy. They also learned how to fly on broomsticks and flying horses during their PE lessons.

Each child had his or her own little bedroom. They thought it was their second home.

Gravity collected the spiderwebs of happiness on his pink memory stick, during their lunchtime. Nobody noticed anything. Then he returned to the castle to talk about the next step.

'Here is a pink memory stick with some happiness from 725 children,' he said, and placed it on a little glass table, in front of Rosella.

'Can you possibly pull out 275 children from other countries around?' she asked and fiddled with the memory stick.

‘Good idea! Of course I can. It might take a few hours, but I can do it today. It needs a lot of energy.’ His wolf showed his teeth again.

‘After you take some happiness from those children, I will turn them into black swans, to hide,’ she said in her mysterious voice.

‘Fabulous!’ they shouted and started to work.

Then, Gravity took one of his grey flying horses and rose above the castle. When he reached the cloud level, he pulled 275 children out of their positions on the ground and placed them gently into Rosella’s garden. After that he ran down on the ground and collected the spiderwebs of happiness.

Finally, he had 1,000 of them on his pink memory stick. Then Rosella performed a complicated charm and weird dance and turned all the children into beautiful black swans and led them to swim on top of her lake.

'Fantastic job,' said Gravity and gave Rosella his pink memory stick.

'I couldn't have done it without your amazing talent, Gravity,' she admitted and gave him a grey, triple magic moonstone.

'Well. Awesome this little gadget will make me even more powerful,' he declared in a happy voice.

'Now I have all the ingredients for my live-forever potion!' Rosella smiled like a child. 'I will start making it as soon as I can. Please join me in the process.' She said goodbye and disappeared in a puff of purple smoke.

Chapter 10

Live-forever potion

That evening, Rosella, Water, Fire, Gravity and Rosella's cat Night gathered around the cauldron, talking about the process. An ancient, scruffy looking, brown magic book floated in front of Rosella.

'Step 1,' she read. 'Place a ring of life in the bottom of an empty cauldron.'

So, with his gravitational powers Gravity put a pulsating, full-of-energy ring of life right in the middle of the empty cauldron.

'Do you know that the ring of life increases everyone's life in the country for 500 years?' he asked everyone.

'This is a nice surprise for my people,' Rosella answered quietly.

'Step 2. Pour in some water and let it boil for a minute,' she read. 'Then place a large pumpkin and two poisoned apples in it.'

Water added some water. Night put in apples and pumpkins. Fire set up a nice steady fire underneath.

'Step 3. Place a pot of the hottest lava on earth into the mixture and boil for six hours.'

Fire added lava and they had a long time to wait. It was almost morning when it was time for the next step.

'Step 4. Sprinkle the positive energy, collected from 1,000 children into the mixture,' Rosella read the instructions and then sprinkled the memories all over.

‘Step 5. If the mixture turns into a nice red colour you can cool it down and drink it,’ Rosella read further.

‘It’s red enough for me,’ said Gravity.

Water took the mixture and gently cooled it down. Then she poured it into a crystal glass.

‘Are you ready, your Majesty?’ she asked the Queen.

‘Yes, I am unquestionably ready. I have waited for this moment my entire life.’

She took a crystal glass raised it, said cheers and drank almost everything before stumbling backwards.

The glass fell out of her hand, but didn’t break, just spilled some liquid. Rosella nearly lost consciousness. Gravity put her on a settee. All the voices in her head were distant and unreal.

In a few minutes she felt stronger and stronger. Then she understood the question and opened her eyes.

'Are you all right, my love?' Fire asked loudly. 'Congratulations for being immortal.'

'Yes, I feel so strong and powerful, like never before.'

She stood up and walked towards him. Suddenly, her cat, Night, jumped across the room and licked the rest of the potion

‘Naughty boy!’ Rosella said in her croaky voice and smiled.

‘Please come to my castle everyone to celebrate!’ Fire proclaimed loudly.

Chapter 11

Marriage proposal

Rosella looked especially beautiful at that moment. She was wearing a maroon, silky dress, which swept on the floor when she walked.

Her eyes sparkled mysteriously and a huge smile was always on her face. They all appeared instantaneously in Fire's pyramid-shaped Royal Hall. It had golden walls and a red slippery marble floor. A large fire burned in a red marble fireplace.

The multiple talking lit candles and mirrors decorated the room. A round, white table for four was prepared exactly in the middle.

Five beautiful firebirds with pink, red, green and blue fire-flamed feathers flew around the Royal Hall, singing sweetly.

Four robot penguins served breakfast, waddling from side to side. Four immortal people sat

around the table, comfortably. The King Fire stood up and gave his royal speech.

'Firstly, we are all gathered here to congratulate Rosella the Queen of The Darkness World with becoming immortal.' Everyone cheered.

'Then, I would like to ask Rosella

to become the Queen of Lavinia, my wife, mother of my children, my Queen and share an eternity together. Rosella would you like to marry me?'

'Yes! I do, your Majesty.' He walked across the room and put a white luminous ring on her finger.

'This ring is made of light,' he explained. 'It is the most expensive ring in our galaxy. It can be white or change colour to any colour of the rainbow at your command.'

'Thank you Fire the Greatest. It is the best day of my life!' She smiled and gave him a hug.

'Congratulations, your Majesty! Here is my wedding present for you. It is a wishing fish. It has seven wishes. After that it has to change master,' Water said smiling and gave Rosella her gift.

'Thank you! It's marvellous. I don't even know what to wish for,' Rosella answered with a grin and gave her a quick glance.

'This is a magical, infinite energy stone,' said Gravity and took out a little grey box. 'It has so much energy, that it can help your spaceship travel faster than the speed of light.' He gave it to Fire.

'Wow!' His eyes round. 'Thank you, Gravity! I have never seen one before.' They shook hands. 'It will definitely become useful, when I take my future wife on my next space trip.' He smiled.

Then, Rosella's cat Night showed his dance routine with ten broomsticks. Press caught a few cakes, making everyone laugh.

Everyone enjoyed themselves during this celebration.

Suddenly, Rosella's mobile mirror spoke loudly.

'The parents and guardians of the children arrived at your castle, destroyed protection charms and demanded their children. Your sisters Snowflake of Bearland and Mary of Philiphia brought them there.'

Rosella stood up, said thank you and goodbye and disappeared in purple smoke.

Chapter 12

Parents and guardians

Rosella put a few extra charms inside the castle and appeared on her royal balcony, wearing a purple dress and a pointy hat. She had a purple wand with her just in case.

'Crazy witch! Where are our children? Give them back or we will destroy your castle!' the people shouted from the crowd.

'Your kids are here!' she started. 'You can destroy my castle, but you can't destroy me because I am immortal.' Her voice sounded strong and loud.

'Liar! Give them back!' someone yelled.

‘As you wish!’ She waved her right hand gracefully and a flock of black swans landed on the ground, beside their parents and turned straight back into kids. All of them except one.

‘Why did you come here Snowflake and Mary?’ Rosella asked her sisters in a loud voice.

'To collect Princess Crystal, Prince Orange and Princess Yellow,' Snowflake replied straightaway.

'What a stupid question. I thought you were clever. Why did you take them?' Mary answered too.

'Do you know what my beloved sisters, I am getting married, but not inviting either of you.'

'Nobody needs your weird

invitations,' Snowflake answered with a trembling voice.

'Go! Now! All of you out of my land and never return, if you don't want a serious conflict.'

Everybody gradually disappeared. Rosella stood on the balcony for a long time like a statue. In the bottom of her heart she felt sad about arguing with her sisters, but she didn't show it. The three of them used to run around the castle laughing, when they were little kids.

All of a sudden, she noticed a single black swan left behind. She came down to the bird and turned it into a child. It was a little lobster girl.

‘What is your name, my dear?’ she asked the child.

‘Adele Lobster, your Majesty,’ she answered bravely back.

‘Where are your parents, my poor little child?’ the Queen asked again.

‘They died when I was a baby. I grew up in an orphanage with all the other kids.’

‘Maybe your principal is looking for you everywhere?’

‘No, she hates me,’ the child replied and started to cry.

‘I have an idea,’ Rosella smiled. ‘Would you like to stay in my boarding school? I can become your parent forever. What do you think about that?'

'Sounds amazing!' She jumped up and down. 'Thank you, your Majesty. You are truly the best.'

Rosella took Adele's hand and walked all the way to her boarding school. She gave the child to the principal and made sure that everything was done for her in the best possible way. Adele received her own little bedroom and was shown around the school.

Chapter 13

Wedding day

They decided to have their wedding day on a little island in the middle of a pink lava lake. The sky looked purple, contrasting with the pink quiet water. The pink flamingos floated gracefully around the lake.

The island had a little golden

pyramid-shaped castle in the middle of the perfect green lawn. The numerous firebirds flew around the island, singing beautiful melodies. The chocolate geysers were here and there, inviting everyone to enjoy. A few tables were outside full of scrumptious, exotic food. There were jumping magic jellies, flying pumpkin pies, mini chocolate broomsticks and pumpkin happiness potion. A few robot penguins served their meals.

The ballroom had golden walls and delicate mirrors throughout and a pink marble floor. The wedding guests looked absolutely fantastic with golden, silver, purple and yellow dresses and suits.

They talked to each other quietly, waiting for the ceremony to begin.

The King Fire was wearing a golden jacket with rubies, a golden royal crown, red trousers and golden long boots. All his family and relations, forces of nature, one god, two angels, witches and wizards were already there. Only the bride was missing.

Finally, she appeared wearing a golden dress with red and yellow flames throughout with a long train behind her. Three little bridesmaids in red helped to carry the train. One of them was Adele. Rosella looked absolutely gorgeous.

Her royal crown sparkled with rubies and diamonds, in contrast with her black hair. She walked towards the King with Gravity. He was wearing a silver suit and a silver air cylinder. The firebirds sung a wedding song.

'I Fire, the King of Lavinia, take you Rosella, the Queen of The Darkness World, to be my lawful wedded wife, in sickness and in health for eternity,' he said proudly.

‘I Rosella, the Queen of The Darkness World, take you King Fire of Lavinia to be my lawful wedded husband, in sickness and in health for eternity,’ she answered him in her croaky voice.

‘I pronounce you husband and wife. You may kiss the bride,’ a white angel said loudly.

They exchanged the rings. Than they had a long passionate kiss. The tons of colourful confetti fell down on the ground for a long time. Then they had an amazing wedding breakfast celebration. The wedding night finished with a broomstick-flying disco under the bright full moon and mysterious stars.

DISCO